LOU'S GAME

If my life were a game, it'd be a little like this:

START

And we're off! You're 12 years old and you set off in life with a head full of dreams.

YAHOO!

That's me, here.

1 Tristan

Lucky you, the boy you've (secretly) liked since kindergarten lives across the street. Roll again.

WOW, HE'S CUTE!

Tristan is completely in love (with his videogame). And anyway, Tristan lives in another town now...

A sort of a cat anyway.

2 Cat

A cat comes in through the window. He makes puppy eyes at your mother. You decide to adopt him.

Make up a dozen stupid names for him before your next turn.

Some cat name examples: PUFF-PUFF DADDY, SLIPPER, MOONFACE, DIGGER, ZIPPY, HYACINTH, DRAPES, YOGURT, JOHNNY DEPP, SOLID SNAKE, LIZARD, STINKAT, MR. MXYZPTLK, SINISTRO, CHICKEN, LORD GAGA, OLD SPICE...

12 Off to MORTSVILLE

Memaw's village in the middle of nowhere.

Hurry! Roll again! You'll miss the train!

13 LOOK OUT!

BRUSSELS SPROUTS

MANDATORY

I know, its cruel, but go back to the start.

14 A LETTER

from Tristan! But a super-dumb letter, and you're super-disappointed.

"STAY COOL"?

HOW ROMANTIC!

Skip two turns while you brood.

3 OH NO! That pig picks his nose!

YUCK!

Umm...but you do too, sometimes, when no one's looking.....Skip a turn.

11 Mom

Your mother hasn't finished her science fiction novel.

ZERO → ← NOTHING ← BLANK ← ZILCH

Stay on this space for three turns!

20 HOME AGAIN

Weirdly, this year you're a little sad to be leaving Mortsville...

But you were sick of Brussels sprouts anyway. Roll again.

21 WHOOT! LOVEBIRDS!

YES!

On the train platform, your mother smooches Richard! Finally! Shout "yes" until your next turn.

22 NOTHING AT ALL

ER... I... UM—UH...

Your mother and Mina surprise you for your birthday and invite Tristan to your party. Turns out that you don't have a lot in common. Skip a turn.

15 Paul is a strange

guy you meet in the country. HIHIHI

With him around, summer in Mortsville seems less long. Move ahead three spaces.

4 A new neighbor

He has weird taste but he seems nice. What if he's the ideal man for your mother?

This is Paul

They say she has eyes under her bangs, but maybe that's just a myth.

loser

A rakes progress

DANCE STEPS
BOOM
CHICKA
BOOM
CHICKA
BOOM
etc. etc. until you fall over.

10 ALONE! Richard's gone to work at a summer camp, and Tristan has moved away without a word.
Sing the blues until your next turn.

9 FIASCO. On the big day, Tristan and your mother are useless.
Have a good sulk and skip a turn.

8 HAPPY DANCE! A Valentine's day card from Tristan for you, and one from Richard for your mother!
Party! Dance like a wild thing and roll again.

19 Clement Fibber — Hit the road, Clem! Your mother gets re-inspired and finally finishes her book!
YEEHAW!
Shout "Clement Fibber is a loser" and roll again.

18 ALOHA! Paul sings you a song. You are enchanted.
Close your eyes and drift until your next turn.

finish — You're 13 years old!
13
(For what it's worth...)

WHAT A DISASTER! You argue with Paul, and your mother accepts a dinner date with a big loser.

7 MEMAW shows up without warning and stays for a week!
A MESS, AS ALWAYS!
Sweep the place clean and skip a turn.

MEMAW LOVES:
— munching Brussels sprouts while watching "Love, Fame, and Beauty."
— cheating at Scrabble.

MEMAW HATES:
— her neighbor
— electronic devices
— music
— oversleeping
— paper towels
— speeches
— yoga
— lazy people
— her neighbor
— sprouts that aren't from Brussels
— bright colors
— Brooke Logan from "Love, Fame, and Beauty"
— the big city
— storekeepers
— old people
— instruction manuals
— bread
— her neighbor
— jokes
— redheads
— disturbances
— artists
— the president
— her neighbor
— people who whine all the time

6 It's raining! DEADLY BOREDOM! You're trapped with Memaw's stupid soaps and interminable Scrabble games.
TRIPLE WORD SCORE
Try to form a word with the letters POCZSULB. If you can't, skip fourteen turns.

17 Apologize and move to the next square.

6 INTRIGUES On the one hand, you have to use all sorts of tricks to get your mom and Richard together, and on the other, you have to get together with Tristan without looking obvious...
All this plotting is exhausting! Take a break, play a videogame or eat some excellent Gino's pizza while waiting for your next turn.

5 Mina, your absolute best friend since kindergarten.
FRIENDS... ...FOR LIFE!
In homage to her legendary vigor, do three pushups.

Richard — YO. OTOH, his vest is gross! Baa like a dying sheep until your next turn!

OOH! WHAT A NICE VEST! WHY DON'T I WEAR IT ALL THE TIME?
BAA BAA BAA
THE VEST MACHINE

My friend, yo!

I'VE BEEN FRIENDS WITH HER SO LONG THAT:
* I can dial her number without looking.
BIP BIP
* We don't need to talk for hours to understand each other...
* But we still talk for hours.

Lou! 3

Down in the Dumps

JULIEN NEEL

GRAPHIC UNIVERSE™ · MINNEAPOLIS · NEW YORK

TO MATHILDE
TO MAMIE AND MONSIEUR PAPA

Story and art by Julien Neel

Translation by Carol Klio Burrell

First American edition published in 2012 by Graphic Universe™.

Lou! by Julien Neel © 2006 — Glénat Editions
© 2012 Lerner Publishing Group, Inc., for the U.S. edition

Graphic Universe™ is a trademark of Lerner Publishing Group, Inc.

Graphic Universe™
A division of Lerner Publishing Group, Inc.
241 First Avenue North
Minneapolis, MN 55401 U.S.A.

Website address: www.lernerbooks.com

Library of Congress Cataloging-in-Publication Data

Neel, Julien.
　　[Cimetière des autobus. English]
　　Down in the dumps / written and illustrated by Julien Neel ; translation by Carol Klio Burrell. — 1st American ed.
　　　p.　cm. — (Lou! ; #3)
　　Summary: Lou finds it confusing and difficult to be thirteen, especially with her mother and Richard's romance heating up, being separated from her best friend Mina at school, and getting another letter from Paul when she never answered the first one.
　　ISBN 978-0-7613-8779-4 (lib. bdg. : alk. paper)
　　[1. Graphic novels 2. Mothers and daughters—Fiction. 3. Best friends—Fiction.
4. Friendship—Fiction. 5. Junior high schools—Fiction. 6. Schools—Fiction.
7. Dating (Social customs)—Fiction. 8. Graphic novels] I. Burrell, Carol Klio. II. Title.
PZ7.7.N44Dow 2012
741.5'944—dc23　　　　　　　　　　　　　　　　　2012003973

Manufactured in the United States of America
1 – DP – 7/15/12

OK. YOU TWO HAVE GONE COMPLETELY, TOTALLY...

...CRAZY.

HEH, WE JUST THOUGHT IT'D BE MORE PRACTICAL...

BETWEEN OUR TWO PLACES...

SEEING AS HOW WE'RE...

...IN LOVE!

HEH!

SO I SEE...

I DUNNO, I GUESS IT'S THE THING TO DO THESE DAYS, TO SYMBOLICALLY SMASH DOWN WALLS...

...I SHOULD ASK MY SHRINK ABOUT IT...

smooch

GRRR

HUH? WHASSAT?

NOTHING, NEVER MIND...

I'M GOING. I HAVE THAT THING, YOU KNOW: FIRST DAY OF SCHOOL...

BYE-EE

HEY!

WHAT'S UP?

I'LL TELL YOU ON THE WAY...

BUT...

...THIS IS SO BOGUS!

...WE AREN'T IN THE SAME CLASS!

THAT STINKS!

10 A 9 A 8 A 7 A
10 B 9 B 8 B
10 C 9 C 8 C 7 C

BOOHOO... LOULOU!

MINAAA! DON'T LET GO!

DRiiiiiiiiNG!

SNIF

THINK OF ME, OK?

P-PROMISE...

SNIF

SEE YOU AT LUNCH, OK?

YEP...

...IF THE GRIEF DOESN'T KILL US FIRST...

YOU WILL BE QUIET AND YOU WILL TAKE YOUR PLACES SILENTLY...

blabla blablabl blablabl

bla bla bla

YOU CAN TALK ABOUT YOUR VACATIONS BETWEEN CLASSES...

Bla bla bla bla

Bla bla bla

bla bla bl

DOES ANYONE HERE WANT TO BE SENT TO THE PRINCIPAL ON THE FIRST DAY?

I HAVE FREE TICKETS!

HEY...COULD YOU SIT SOMEWHERE ELSE...THAT'S MY BEST FRIEND...

WE'VE SAT TOGETHER SINCE FIRST GRADE...

OH, SURE...

I UNDERSTAND...

QUIET, I TOLD YOU...

AND TAKE YOUR SEAT NOW...

I WILL BE YOUR HOMEROOM TEACHER THIS YEAR...

ANYONE SITTING HERE?

NOPE.

THOSE REPEATING THIS CLASS ALREADY KNOW MY NICKNAME: THE PREDATOR!

TAKE OUT A SHEET OF PAPER. WRITE YOUR LAST NAME, FIRST NAME, AND LAST WISHES...

YOUR OUTFIT'S COOL.

I'M LOU.

LOU. THAT'S COOL. IT'S SHORT. I'M MARY EMILY. STUPID NAME...

OH, NO, IT'S NICE.

ARE YOU NEW HERE?

YEAH...BUT I WON'T BE HERE LONG...

AS SOON AS I CAN, I'M OUT OF HERE. MY BOYFRIEND SELLS SHARK TOOTH NECKLACES TO TOURISTS. WHEN HE MAKES ENOUGH MONEY, I'M DITCHING MY PARENTS AND WE'RE HITTING THE ROAD...

SHARK TOOTH NECKLACES? WOW, CLASSY...

YUP.

WANT ONE?

HUH? UH, NO...I...

I'M TRYING TO QUIT...

COOL. GOOD FOR YOU.

DO YOU HAVE A BOYFRIEND?

WELL, NOT REALLY. THAT IS, IT'S A LITTLE COMPLICATED. THERE WAS THIS BOY WHO AND...

YES, YOU HAVE THE RIGHT IDEA. YOU'RE FREE.

?

ANYWAY, GUYS ARE ALL JERKS...

YUP.

DRiiiiiiiiiiiiiiiiiNG!

FORGET ABOUT 'EM.

YEAH, FORGET ABOUT 'EM.

OK, SEE YOU TOMORROW.

YEAH, SURE. IF I HAVEN'T GOTTEN EXPELLED YET.

WHOA.

HEY, MINA!

SO...ARE YOU MAD AT ME OR WHAT?

GET LOST. SHE DOESN'T WANT TO TALK TO YOU.

HIPPIE!

HIPPIE? WHAT ARE YOU--

HAVE YOU SEEN YOUR OUTFIT? THE SIXTIES ARE OVER, WEIRDO.

THAT'S ENOUGH. LET'S GO...

HAVE YOU SEEN THAT RAPPER WANNABE GETUP YOU'RE WEARING?

ARE YOU STARTING SOMETHING? ARE YOU STARTING SOMETHING?

C'MON, CALM DOWN!

TRAMP!

TRASH!

♪LOULOU!♪

HIYA!

HOW SWEET, MAW AND PAW HAVE COME TO GET HER SO SHE CAN GO HERD THE SHEEP.

7

YOU'D **NEVER** TREAT J. K. ROWLING LIKE THAT!

MRMPF!

HMFRPFR!

MRPFPFF!

ANYTHING IN PARTICULAR YOU'D LIKE, TO MAKE THIS CELEBRATION MORE DIGNIFIED?

HMMM... LET'S SEE...

HEY, GINO, THERE'S SOMETHING I ALWAYS WANTED TO ASK YOU...

GINO PIZZA

THAT GIANT BOTTLE OF CHIANTI OVER THERE... IS IT REAL OR JUST FOR DECORATION?

DECORATION.

WOW.

KRONFE...

RFZZR...

RRPFZBL...

BIDLING
CHINC
DING
BIBLING
DIGLING
BLING
GLING
BLING
GLING

UGGGGHH...
WHAT'S ALL
THE RACKET?

SHHH, IT'S NOTHING,
GO BACK TO SLEEP...

?

I'M BORROWING
YOUR VINTAGE
BIKER BOOTS,
OK?

BYE.

HUH? WHATEVER YOU
WANT, BUT PLEASE,
DON'T SLAM THE DOOR!

SBLAM!

OW, MY
HEAD.

A BUS CEMETERY.

RIGHT ACROSS FROM ME.

WHERE TRISTAN WAS...

ALL TORN DOWN.

THE BUILDING, NOT TRISTAN.

TRISTAN, YOU KNOW, THE BOY WHO...

...WHO MOVED TO ANOTHER CITY.

AND WHO I REALLY LIKED AND THEN ZIP...

NOT A PEEP.

I DON'T KNOW WHY.

I...

ANYWAY...

THERE'S THIS OTHER BOY.

PAUL.

WHO I MET AT MEMAW'S...

BUT WE DON'T LIKE EACH OTHER THAT WAY.

I DON'T THINK SO, ANYWAY...

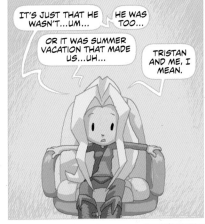

IT'S JUST THAT HE WASN'T...UM...

HE WAS TOO...

OR IT WAS SUMMER VACATION THAT MADE US...UH...

TRISTAN AND ME, I MEAN.

ANYWAY, YOU SEE, THAT IS--NO: FOR EXAMPLE, MY MOTHER...

AND RICHARD...

OUR NEIGHBOR.

THE OTHER ONE.

THERE THEY ARE.

BOOM.

IN LOVE!

...AND THAT AWFUL CLEMENT FIFFER.

HEHE!

SO, THEY KNOCKED DOWN THE WALL BETWEEN OUR APARTMENTS.

THAT WAS A SHOCK.

THEN THE FIRST DAY OF SCHOOL.

BLAH! AND THEN AT SCHOOL, BLAH BLAH BLAH...

I HAD A HUGE FIGHT WITH MINA.

I DON'T EVEN KNOW IF WE'RE STILL FRIENDS...

ANYWAY, ALL OF THIS, I DUNNO, IT'S LIKE...

I SORT OF FEEL LIKE...

UM...

HOW TO SAY IT...

CONFUSED?

THAT'S IT!

RENT!

OOOOOOOH, LOOK WHO IT IS! MRS. WARD!

WHAT A... PLEASURE.

IMAGINE MEETING YOU HERE, WHAT LUCK! BECAUSE...

...ABOUT THE RENT...

...YOU'LL GET A KICK OUT OF THIS.

YOU KNOW MY BOOK... SO, IT'S ON SALE NOW...

SO, RIGHT, THE MONEY...

YOU'VE HEARD OF J. K. ROWLING?

SOOO, ONE OF THESE DAYS THAT COULD BE ME

RENT!

YES YES YES

LOOK! OPRAH WINFREY!

WHERE? WHERE?

DARNIT. GOT ME AGAIN WITH THE OL' OPRAH WINFREY TRICK.

14

Aloha, friend!
We said we'd write and all that,
so here I go...

I won't bore you with stories about school. Like always, the jerks are messing with me, and like always, I couldn't care less...

I read your mom's book and really loved it. I started putting lots of science fiction stuff in my paintings and my Polynesian songs...

My wahinas are wearing space helmets, and there are extraterrestrial crabs and space rovers overrun by jungle vines...

The tiki statues are the traces of ancient visitors. The ocean and the cosmos are all mixed up. I wish you could see it all!

I'd love to watch the falling starfish with you...

PAUL...

HEY, I KNOW! LET'S PUT ON SOME DUMB MUSIC AND DANCE!

UH...NO.

OR LET'S MAKE A LIST OF GIRLS AND GUYS, AND THEN FIGURE OUT THE BEST COUPLES.

THAT'D BE FUN.

YEAH, IF WE WERE ELEVEN YEARS OLD...

LET'S JUST KEEP WATCHING TV.

BiDi BiDi BiDi ♫

YEAH, HELLO?

?

HELLOOOO?

BIP

17

18

...AND THEN THERE'S THIS BOY, PAUL, WHO I MET AT MY GRANDMOTHER'S, IN THE COUNTRY. SURE, HE'S A LITTLE OLDER THAN I A

YOU HUNGRY?

SLAM!

SLAM! SLAM! SLAM!

UH...WON'T THAT WAKE YOUR PARENTS?

MY PARENTS CAN GET LOST!

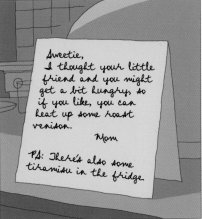

Sweetie,
I thought your little friend and you might get a bit hungry, so if you like, you can heat up some roast venison.

Mom

P.S: There's also some tiramisu in the fridge.

YAY, ROAST VENISON.

GROSS.

CRITCH CRITCH

THE POWER OF THE DARK SIDE UNDERESTIMATE YOU MUST NOT.

HEHE HEHE!

WHERE ARE YOU GOING?

TO CHECK IF THEY'RE TALKING ABOUT MY BOOK ON THE INTERNET!

SLURP.

AW, TOO BAD, IT'S GOTTEN COLD NOW.

HEY! DARKOVERLORD GAVE SIDERA FOUR OUT OF FIVE LIGHTSABERS ON SCIFIGEEKERY.COM!

FOUR LIGHTSABERS! YEEHAW!

HEHE!

WHUMP!

LIKE, Y'KNOW, I BROKE UP WITH THIS GUY BECAUSE HE WAS TOO LAME, Y'KNOW, LIKE, WITH HIS FRIENDS HE PLAYED IT ALL TOUGH THEN AROUND HIS PARENTS HE WENT ALL WIMPY, AND THEN MENTALLY HE'S JUST NOT AT MY LEVEL, Y'KNOW, LIKE, I THOUGHT HE WAS A TOTAL HYPOCRITE AND, LIKE, I'M NOT LIKE THAT, I SPEAK RIGHT UP ABOUT STUFF OTHER PEOPLE DON'T DARE SAY AND, Y'KNOW, I DON'T CARE WHAT SOCIETY THINKS...

THEY CAN'T DEAL WITH REBELS LIKE ME, CHE GUEVARA, OR LADY GAGA...

MUSKAR WAS A WISE KING WHO LIVED IN PEACE WITH HIS NEIGHBORS...

HE DIED IN 1168, MOURNED BY HIS SUBJECTS, AND HIS SON SUCCEEDED HIM AS MUSKAR II. HE WAS TOO WEAK TO MAINTAIN ORDER IN THE COUNTRY AND AN AGE OF ANARCHY REPLACED THE PERIOD OF PROSPERITY...

ANARCHY RULZ!

GUYS DON'T UNDERSTAND ANYTHING ABOUT HOW A GIRL THINKS, YOU KNOW HOW THEY'RE ALWAYS, LIKE, "YO, LADIES," LIKE THEY HAVE NO RESPECT.

AND REALLY I WANT THEM TO RESPECT ME JUST AS I AM, Y'KNOW. BUT IT'S, LIKE, BECAUSE I'M NOT IN THE NORM, I'M A PAIN IN THEIR TINY LITTLE LIVES.

...BUT THEY CAN GET LOST...

HEY!

I **NEED** A HUG, BUDDY.

SORRY...

?

EEEK

PFFFFFT...

IT'S LIKE, LITTLE BY LITTLE, THE THINGS AND PEOPLE AROUND ME ARE GETTING HAZY...

I CAN'T FOCUS ON ANYTHING. THE WORLD IS IMMATERIAL...

NO MORE ROAD BUMPS, NO HIGHS, NO LOWS, EVERYTHING IS FLAT...

I CAN SPEND HOURS LOOKING AT A CRACK IN THE CEILING, BUT I CAN'T READ A BOOK MORE THAN A COUPLE OF SECONDS...

I DON'T KNOW IF EVERYONE ELSE IS TURNING INTO GHOSTS...

...OR IF IT'S ME WHO, LITTLE BY LITTLE, IS JUST TURNING INTO A SHADOW...

...SO INSUBSTANTIAL THAT I FEEL LIKE I'M FLOATING...

LIGHT...

SO LIGHT...

WOW.

LEATHER WRISTBANDS...

...WITH SPIKES...

THAT IS SO COOL...

WHEN I WAS YOUNGER, I DREAMED OF HAVING ONE LIKE THAT.

BUT MY PARENTS, MORTSVILLE, ALL THAT...

ONE WRISTBAND, S'IL VOUS PLAIT.

WITH SPIKES.

EXCELLENT CHOICE.

HEY, NO, WAIT, NO!

MERRY CHRISTMAS!

BUT IT'S SILLY, IT'S...

IT'S...IT'S COOOOOL!

WOW! IT REALLY MAKES ME FEEL TOUGH...

SHH! THE RENT...

RENT?

YEEHAH!

MY GOODNESS!

HEY!

PFFFFF...

HEY, YOU'RE A GUY. SAY THERE'S A GIRL YOU MET ON VACATION, SAY...

OK?

OK, SHE'S JUST A FRIEND. BUT SAY THAT, LATER, SHE GOES BACK HOME, AND YOU WRITE HER A LETTER...

A LETTER? WHAT KIND OF LETTER?

JUST A LETTER: "DEAR WHOSITS, HOW'S IT GOING," AND SO ON AND SO FORTH...

OK, GOT IT...AND?

...AND THIS GIRL DOESN'T ANSWER FOR MONTHS.

UGH, SHE'S AWFUL!

NO, NO, NO. IT'S NOT THAT SHE'S BAD. IT'S THAT SHE'S PARALYZED WITH FEAR, AND SHE'S AFRAID TO WRITE SOMETHING DUMB AND LOOK LIKE A MORON...

SO...

SHE DOESN'T REPLY, BUT AT CHRISTMAS, YOU SEND A CARD ANYWAY...

WELL, THEN, I'M REALLY NICE TO DO THAT, CONSIDERING THAT SHE DIDN'T WRITE BACK THE FIRST TIME...

YEAH, THAT'S WHAT THE GIRL THINKS TOO. THAT YOU'RE SUPER NICE AND THAT SHE HAS TO WRITE BACK OR RISK LOSING YOU AS A FRIEND...

THING IS, IT'S THAT SHE DOESN'T KNOW HOW TO EXPLAIN WHY SHE DIDN'T REPLY BEFORE...

SO...SHE FINALLY WRITES YOU:

"DEAR FRIEND, I'M SORRY I DIDN'T ANSWER YOUR FIRST LETTER. I HAD ALL THIS STUFF HAPPENING WITH THE MAFIA, WHO BROKE ALL MY FINGERS. ANYWAY, I GOT BETTER. MERRY CHRISTMAS AND BEST WISHES..."

UH...I DON'T THINK THAT MAFIA STORY HOLDS UP.

THAT'S WHAT I THOUGHT...SO I HAVE THIS OTHER IDEA ABOUT BEING ABDUCTED BY SPACE ALIENS...

WHAT KIND OF SPACE ALIENS?

cRiiiTCH!

HEY.

WHAT?

NEXT PERIOD.

YEAH?

WE'RE CUTTING.

HUH? OH, UH...

OK, SURE.

I KNOW A GOOD HIDEOUT.

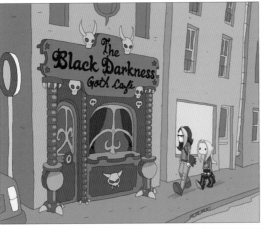

The Black Darkness Goth Café

ESPRESSO.

UH...ME TOO.

SO, YOU KNOW THAT BOY, PAUL, I TOLD YOU ABOUT? HE WROTE ME, AND I HAVEN'T WRITTEN BACK YET...

YEAH, YEAH, Y'KNOW, GUYS ARE ALL THE SAME...

FOR EXAMPLE, I BROKE UP WITH THAT GUY WHO DOES HENNA TATTOOS, HE WAS ALWAYS FREAKING OUT ABOUT STUFF, LIKE I CARE ABOUT HIS LITTLE PROBLEMS. Y'KNOW, IF YOU LOOK AT WHAT'S GOING ON IN THE WORLD, IT'LL TOTALLY MESS YOU UP...

IT'S LIKE AMERICANS THINK WE'RE THE MASTERS OF THE WORLD, WHEN WE'RE REALLY SELLING WEAPONS FOR OIL, BUT IN THE END ALL GOVERNMENTS ARE ALL COMPLETE FAKE LIARS...

AND, Y'KNOW, I CAN'T STAND INJUSTICE, EVEN MORE THAN POVERTY, FRANKLY, SO I DON'T WANT TO GO TO WORK AT SOME FACTORY LIKE A SHEEP, Y'KNOW. AND THAT'S WHAT GETS ALL UP IN THE MAN'S FACE, BECAUSE I WON'T BE A PART OF THE SYSTEM...

SHUT UP!

UM...

I... I...

Black Darkness Goth Café

27

KSHLUNK
KSHLUNK

BiP BiP
BiP

HELLO?

HELLOOO?

MOM?

WHAT DO YOU MEAN, YOU CAN'T HEAR?

TURN IT AROUND!

HOLD THE PHONE THE OTHER SIDE UP!

IT'S WORKING?

YOU OK?

GOOD.

RIGHT, THE ARTHRITIS.

YES, YES.

YES, IT'S A PAIN, YES.

YES, THAT TOO, YES.

AND THE VARICOSE VEINS, OF COURSE...

YOU SAW THE DOCTOR?

OF COURSE I REMEMBER CLEMENT FIFFER...

HUH?

WE'RE NOT GOING BACK OVER THAT AGAIN, ARE WE?

YEAH, YEAH SO, YOU KNOW MY BOOK THAT I WROTE...?

...WELL, IT CAME OUT.

YES.

HUH?

I DON'T CARE THAT MRS. BIGGINS'S GRANDSON GOT HIS ENGINEERING DEGREE!

I WROTE A BOOK GOSHDARNIT!

FINE, THEN CONGRATULATE HER FOR ME!

BYE!

BiP.

RAAAAAAAAAAAAAAA

PWOF

GRUMBLLGRUMBLLL . . .

CLANG.

YOU... YOU...

NO TIME!

THIS BOOK RIGHT HERE!

MY DAUGHTER WROTE IT!

I'LL TAKE TWENTY.

29

♪ SOUP'S ON ♪

CHOW TIME

IT'S READY!

♪ LAAAADIES? ♪

HEY.

MMM?

JUST SPOKE WITH YOUR MOTHER?

SHH

GO FIND YOUR DAUGHTER. TIME TO EAT.

RIGHTO.

LOULOU?

IT'S SUP-SUP-SUPPERTIME!

SHE ISN'T HERE.

CALL HER CELL.

RIGHT.

TUTUTUTU

BIDIBIDIBIDIBI

OH, WAIT, HER PHONE'S RIGHT HERE.

BIDIBIDI BIDIBI

THAT'S STRANGE.

SHE NEVER LEAVES WITHOUT IT.

MAYBE SHE'S AT A FRIEND'S?

I DON'T THINK SHE SAID SHE WAS GOING OUT.

SHE SAY ANYTHING TO YOU?

HEY! I'M FREAKING OUT HERE!

WILL YOU STOP EATING?!

LOU?

LOOOU?

HOLD ON, CALM DOWN. WE'LL PHONE HER FRIENDS.

32

S-SO, DOCTOR...?

W-WHAT DOES SHE HAVE?

A RUNNY NOSE AND A RAGING FEVER. IT'S A BAD CASE OF FLU. NO PROBLEM, I'VE WRITTEN YOU A PRESCRIPTION...

TWO WEEKS OF BED REST!

BUT...THE OTHER THING...

OTHER THING?

I CAN'T DO ANYTHING ABOUT IT.

SEVERE ADOLESCENT CRISIS.

SO.

THAT'S THAT.

THIRTY DOLLARS COPAY.

CRISIS WHAT?

WAIT, ARE YOU SURE, ABOUT THE SECOND THING, THERE ISN'T SOMETHING...?

A PILL, MAYBE?

SNIF

HEY.

HEY.

SNIF

HMM, YOU DON'T LOOK SO GOOD.

NOPE.

YOU TALK NOW?

HA HA HA! IMAGINE: A TALKING CAT! NOPE, YOU'RE HALLUCINATING!

IT'S THE FEVER! HA!

OH, OK.

SNIF

HOW DID THIS HAPPEN? HOW DID THIS HAPPEN? I...I DIDN'T SEE IT COMING...JUST YESTERDAY SHE WAS SO LITTLE, AND THEN...WHAM!

TEENAGER.

I'M A TOTAL FAILURE, EVER SINCE SHE WAS A BABY. BUT I TRIED TO DO EVERYTHING RIGHT. MAKE SURE SHE NEVER WANTED FOR ANYTHING, THAT SHE WAS HAPPY...AND...

I, UH...I DON'T KNOW...RAISING A KID, IT'S, UM...LIKE STAR WARS...JEDI TRAINING...SO, YOU HAVE TO BE LIKE OBI-WAN, AND SHE'S LIKE ANAKIN...

OH, NO, WAIT: YOU'RE YODA, AND...

HUH?

NO, I KNOW: ADOLESCENCE IS LIKE WHEN SUPERMAN IS ADOPTED BY THE KENTS AND WHEN HE GROWS UP DISCOVERS THAT HE'S FROM KRYPTON, SO HE DECIDES TO GO LIVE IN METROPOLIS...UH...NO...

NOT LIKE THAT, ACTUALLY...

I DON'T THINK I'M THE RIGHT PERSON TO TALK ABOUT THIS STUFF. ALL I'VE GOT ARE MY STUPID SUPERHERO STORIES...UH...I THINK THAT, AS A MOM, YOU'RE AWESOME. LOU IS BRIGHT AND CREATIVE, AND NOW THAT SHE'S A TEENAGER, OF COURSE THERE'S GONNA BE STUFF YOU DON'T UNDERSTAND...

...AND THIS IS A JOURNEY SHE HAS TO TAKE ON HER OWN.

...I BELIEVE.

YOU'RE NICE.

BUT BACK TO STAR WARS. I'D BE MORE LIKE QUI-GON JINN, RIGHT?

THE NECESSARY PASSAGE BETWEEN CHILDHOOD AND ADULTHOOD, ADOLESCENCE OPENS BROAD AND UNKNOWN HORIZONS, STREWN WITH PITFALLS: SELF-AFFIRMATION, CHOOSING A CAREER, EMOTIONAL GROWTH, ETC. IT BRINGS A FAREWELL TO CHILDHOOD AND DETACHMENT FROM ONE'S PARENTS...

I'M DIZZY.

THE ADOLESCENT IS LIKE A LOBSTER THAT, HAVING LOST ITS SHELL, HAS TO HIDE UNDER ROCKS UNTIL IT HAS GROWN A NEW ONE. VULNERABLE TO ALL SORTS OF TRICKY PROPOSITIONS, THE ADOLESCENT SOMETIMES COMPENSATES FOR DEFENSELESSNESS WITH MOOD SWINGS, ACTING OUT, EVEN DEVIANT BEHAVIOR...

BE QUIET.

THE ADOLESCENT ISN'T ALONE IN THIS BEWILDERING TRANSITION. OFTEN, THIS PHASE IS MARKED BY DEEP QUESTIONING BY THE WHOLE FAMILY. SOME PEOPLE ARE NOT ABLE TO FIND THE INNER RESOURCES TO WEATHER THIS. IT CAN RESULT IN NUMEROUS DIFFICULTIES, WHICH SOCIETY ATTEMPTS TO RESOLVE WITH...

SHUDDUP.

HEY.

HEY.

HERE YOU GO. I MADE SOUP WITH CHICKEN BREAST, AND HERE'S YOUR MEDICINE.

HA HA HA HA!

?

WHAT IS IT?

CHICKEN--! HA HA HA HA!

YES.

SO...?

MOM?

YES?

COULD YOU TELL THE CAT TO STOP TALKING ALL THE TIME SO I CAN GET SOME SLEEP?

HUH?

YES, AND THEN IT'D BE NICE IF YOU COULD REPAINT MY ROOM WITH STRAWBERRY JAM.

IT KEEPS THE WILD ANIMALS AWAY.

AH.

YOU STILL HAVE A REALLY HIGH FEVER.

OH, YES, ABSOLUTELY. I WON THE GOLF TOURNAMENT AT FISH-ON-FIGGLE THREE TIMES AND I...

AH! MY DEAR CLEMENT FIFFER!

MY FAVORITE PATIENT!

YOU KNOW, MY DEAR, DR. FIFFER IS THE GREATEST REGIONAL SPECIALIST IN BLOOD CIRCULATION PROBLEMS.

OH MY.

YES, I--

JUST LAST WEEK I HAD LYMPHATIC INFLAMMATION IN MY CALVES, AND MY VARICOSE VEINS WERE PAINING ME TERRIBLY. WELL, OUR DOCTOR HERE MASSAGED ME FOR THREE FULL HOURS. YOU SHOULD HAVE SEEN IT...

IT WAS OOZING EVERYWHERE!

I GOT IT ALL OVER MY HANDS, AND...

MISS? ARE YOU FEELING OK?

YOU'VE GONE PALE...

BYE, CLEMENT, DEAR!

HEH HEH!

LETTUCE! GET YER GORGEOUS LETTUCE HERE!

FRESH FISH! FRESH FISH!

HMMM...

SCIENCE FICTION! SCIIIIENCE FICTION!

GUY DEGRENNE JR. HIGH

HEY.

HEY.

COULD WE MAYBE TALK A LITTLE?

FINE. SURE.

NOT THAT I LIKE YOU OR ANYTHING. BUT IT'S FOR LOU.

YEAH. RIGHT.

YOU KNOW. HER WEIRD RUNNING AWAY AND ALL THAT...

HER MOTHER CALLED ME, TOO, YEAH.

I'M GOING TO SEE HER AT 6.

I HAVE THE NOTES FROM CLASS FOR HER. I'LL GO WITH YOU.

I'M COMING TOO.

MINA!

HELLO!

AND, UM...MARY-WHOSITS...

YOU I DON'T KNOW.

AND, UH...

SO, UM, SHE'S THAT WAY... YOU KNOW...

I'LL LET YOU...

OH, RIGHT! TELL ME, WHILE YOU'RE HERE...

ANYONE KNOW ANYTHING ABOUT ADOLESCENCE?? 'CAUSE I'M DROWNING HERE...

WHY ARE YOU LOOKING AT ME LIKE THAT?

I'M FINE! I'M NOT GOING ANYWHERE!

RIGHT, IT'S JUST...

I MEAN...

YEAH...YOU COULD SAY IT WAS A LITTLE BIT OUR FAULT THAT...

THAT WHAT?

WELL, IF YOU...IF YOU'D...

IF YOU DIDN'T GET BETTER AND ALL, WE...

IT'S BECAUSE OF MY ANNOYING RANTS AND...

IT'S BECAUSE OF MY MOODY TEMPER...

HEY, ARE YOU KIDDING?

C'MON, GIRLS. YOU DIDN'T DO ANYTHING! IT'S ALL IN YOUR HEAD!

SO IT'S A LITTLE TRUE ABOUT THE MOODY TEMPER AND THE ANNOYING RANTS...BUT THAT HAD NOTHING TO DO WITH IT. I JUST...

I DON'T KNOW HOW TO SAY THIS...

I HAD A... LITTLE FREAK-OUT...

THIS BIG EMPTINESS. I FEEL A WHOLE LOT BETTER NOW. BUT IT WAS LIKE I ALWAYS FELT LIKE CRYING...

I DUNNO...

LIKE I WAS WAITING FOR SOMETHING TO HAPPEN...

AND THEN NOTHING...

NOTHING AT ALL...

NOTHING BUT A SORT OF MISERABLE VOID...

BUT...

I DON'T KNOW IF YOU GET IT...

YES, I COMPLETELY GET IT.

YUCK!

SO, DR. FREUD, WHAT DO YOU HAVE TO SAY ABOUT PEOPLE WHO LICK THEIR REARS TO GET CLEAN?

MEOW.

I'M CURED!

DO YOU WANT TO TALK ABOUT... UM...

WHAT?

UH...THIS ADOLESCENCE THING... THERE ARE SOME THINGS WE SHOULD GO OVER, MAYBE...

OH, UM, NO. I DON'T KNOW WHAT HAPPENED. ANYWAY, I THINK I'M BETTER NOW.

I SHOULD BE SAYING SOME REASSURING WORDS TO YOU. THAT'S WHAT PARENTS ARE SUPPOSED TO DO, I GUESS. BUT NOTHING'S COMING TO ME...

I JUST REMEMBER THAT I WAS LIKE THIS AT YOUR AGE...

AND I REMEMBER JUST WHAT IT WAS LIKE...

THE ONLY THING I FEEL LIKE I CAN DO IS KEEP LOVING YOU VERY MUCH...

ANYWAY, THERE'S NO MAGIC FORMULA TO FIX EVERYTHING. NO ONE ANSWER, I THINK. I STILL HAVEN'T FIGURED IT OUT...

MAYBE IT SHOULDN'T BE FIGURED OUT...

THAT'S OK WITH ME.

THIS MIGHT COME IN HANDY.

THE BANK ACCOUNT!

MONEY!

MY BOOK...THE...

AUTHOR ROYALTIES!

AAAAAAAHH!

RENT!

SMACK!

YEEHAW!

...AND THEN HE TELLS ME THAT I'M NOT A TRUE ACTIVIST, AND THAT IF I DON'T WANT TO GO OUT WITH HIM, IT'S MY OWN BAD KARMA. SO I TOLD HIM I WASN'T A HYPOCRITE LIKE HIM, AND HE COULD GO BACK HOME TO HIS MOMMY AND GO PLAY WITH HIS DUMB DJEMBE DRUMS AND TAKE HIS WACKO THEORIES...

...ANYWAY, I DON'T CARE. I'M HOOKING UP WITH MY BOYFRIEND AGAIN. MY **REAL** BOYFRIEND. HE SELLS CHURROS TO TOURISTS DURING THE DAY, BUT AT NIGHT HE PLAYS DIDGERIDOO AROUND A BONFIRE AND...

CAN YOU BELIEVE IT? THEY'RE HANGING OUT TOGETHER.

YEAH...AND HERE I AM GOING ON ABOUT MY LITTLE PROBLEMS...

...BLAH BLAH...

IS...IS THIS WHERE THE BRUNCH IS?

WHAT, THE BARBECUE? OH, YEAH, IT'S HERE...

WANT A WEENIE?

UM, YES, I...WHAT AN... ORIGINAL IDEA FOR A PARTY...

CAN I GET YOU A SODA?

HEY, MARY-WHOSITS! YOUR MOM IS HERE!

RATS.

SO, YOU...WRITE NOVELS?

YEP...WELL, ONE NOVEL SO FAR.

I ADOOORE NOVELS!

AH.

CRUNCH!

OOOOOH, THIS "WEENIE" IS DELIGHTFUL...

...IT'S JUST A HOT DOG...

I ADOOORE IT!

I AM SOOO HAPPY THAT MARY EMILY FINALLY HAS SOME LITTLE FRIENDS...

SHE'S SUCH A SOLITARY CHILD, I...

OH, WE DRINK RIGHT FROM THE BOTTLE?

SAY...I HAVE AN IDEA...WE RENT A HUUUUUGE BEACH HOUSE EVERY YEAR. MAYBE YOU THREE WOULD LIKE TO JOIN US?

THERE'S PLENTY OF ROOM AND A HUUUUUGE POOL!

ALL OF US?

A POOL?

ARRGH, MOM, SHH! YOU'RE EMBARRASSING ME.

ON THE BEACH?

SAY YES! SAY YES! SAY YES! SAY YES!

PUH-LEEZE! I SWEAR ON MY MOTHER'S GRAVE I'LL BE GOOD!

I AM YOUR MOTHER!

PUH-LEEZE! PUH-LEEZE! PUH-LEEZE! PUH-LEEZE! PUH-LEEZE! PUH-LEEZE! PUH-LEEZE!

WELL, IT MIGHT BE OK.

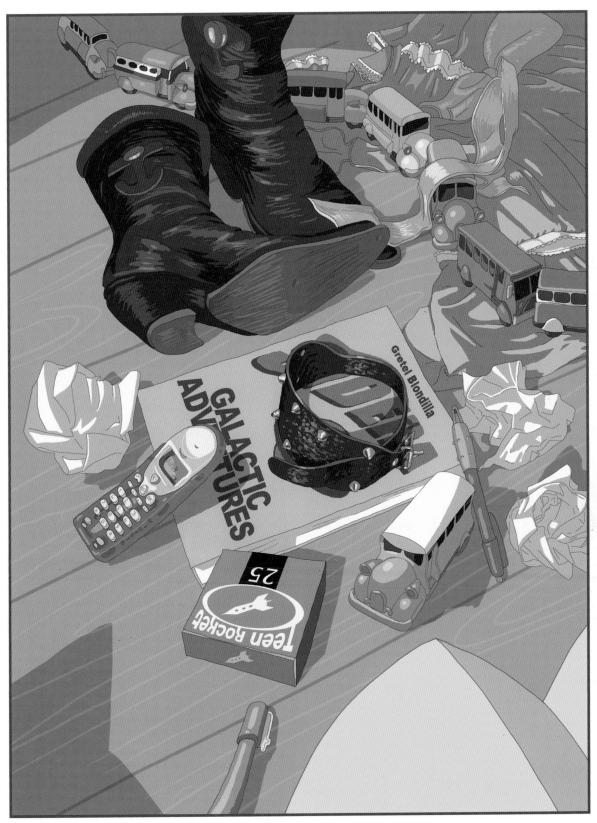

The original back cover of the French edition

mAry EMily

Mary Emily is a girl with REALLY BIG problems. For example, her room is so huge that, this one time, she got lost in it.

YEAH, IT'S LIKE, YOU KNOW...

STICK IT TO THE MAN, YOU KNOW.

NOTE: Actually, she's really fun. It's just that, sometimes, you have to tell her:

SHUT UP!

and after that, she's normal for a few hours.

Actually this look means:
"Somebody love me, please."

KAREN

At first, Karen and me didn't exactly hit it off.
    But in the end, we had a good talk and...well, now she's a friend.

So, in any case, it'd be in our best interests to get along, them, Mina, and me, since we're going on VACATION together this summer!

I CAN'T WAIT!

A sensible girl is hidden under that tracksuit. Any idea how to find her?

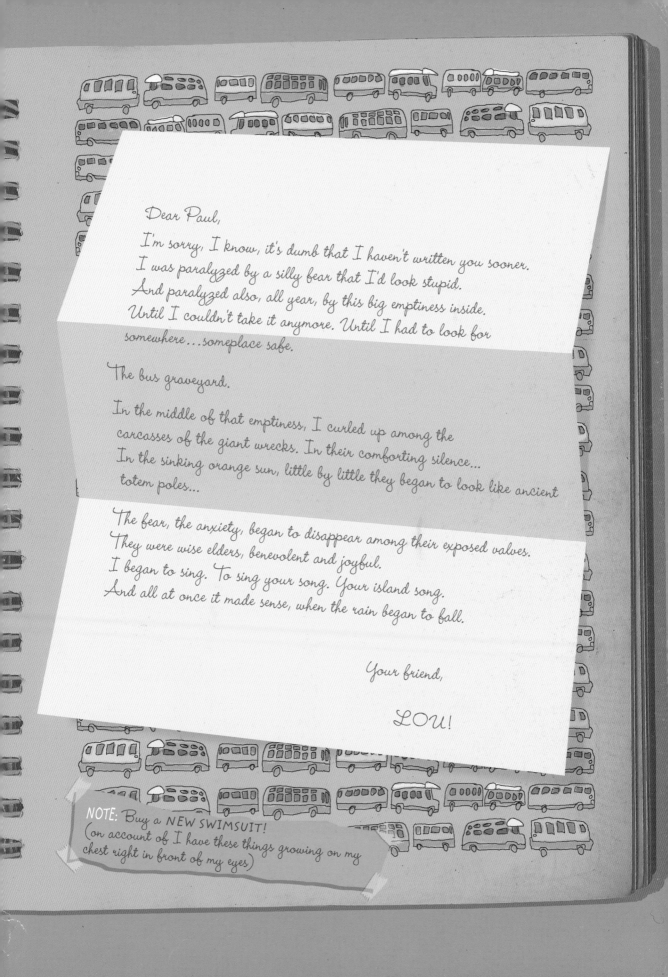

Dear Paul,

I'm sorry, I know, it's dumb that I haven't written you sooner.
I was paralyzed by a silly fear that I'd look stupid.
And paralyzed also, all year, by this big emptiness inside.
Until I couldn't take it anymore. Until I had to look for somewhere...someplace safe.

The bus graveyard.

In the middle of that emptiness, I curled up among the carcasses of the giant wrecks. In their comforting silence...
In the sinking orange sun, little by little they began to look like ancient totem poles...

The fear, the anxiety, began to disappear among their exposed valves.
They were wise elders, benevolent and joyful.
I began to sing. To sing your song. Your island song.
And all at once it made sense, when the rain began to fall.

Your friend,

LOU!

NOTE: Buy a NEW SWIMSUIT!
(on account of I have these things growing on my chest right in front of my eyes)